Kitty's Friends

Bel Mooney

Illustrated by Margaret Chamberlain

EGMO

For Fred Dimbleby

First published in Great Britain 2003
by Egmont Books Limited,
239 Kensington High Street, London W8 6SA

Text copyright © 2003 Bel Mooney
Illustrations copyright © 2003 Margaret Chamberlain

ISBN 1 4052 0585 7

1 3 5 7 9 10 8 6 4 2

A CIP catalogue record for this title
is available from the British Library

Printed in Great Britain
by Cox & Wyman Ltd, Reading, Berkshire

Contents

There are 12 brilliant titles in the

Kitty and friends series.

Collect them all!

I don't want to!
I can't find it!
It's not fair!
But you promised!
Why not?
I know!
I'm scared!
I wish!
Why me?
I'm bored!
It's not my fault!
So what!

Kitty's Friends
A letter from Kitty

Dear Everybody,

Are your friends very important to you? Mine are to me. Sometimes Mum says I fuss too much about them. I don't think that's true.

But it is true that I get very upset if I fall out with somebody. There are days when the person you thought was your very best - or at least nearly very best friend - is a bit mean, and you just don't understand why. Then you feel pretty horrible, until the time (usually the next day!) you go into school, and it's just like it never happened!

It's all right for my little brother, Tom, because babies just eat mushy stuff and glug milk and say 'Goo' and 'Mumma' and the whole world loves them. They don't need friends because all they care about is that mushy stuff and milk and Mum and Dad, and maybe the blue bunny who lives in the cot with them and so is definitely their bestest friend. Easy for Bunny and Baby because neither of them can speak...

Anyway, the rest of us need our friends – and that's why Bel has written these stories all about *my* friends and more or less left me out of them! You can find out about the day William changed, and how Rosie learnt *not* to win, and Anita got fed up with her little brothers (who doesn't?), and how our new friend Tim gave up his old toy and oh, but I shouldn't give it away, should I? As for my cousin Melissa – well,

Kitty's Friends

she's getting to be nearly as naughty as me,
which has got to be good! And in the final story
you'll find *me* in the starring role. As the GUs
sometimes say, we saved the best 'til last.

Love,

Kitty

William

Tim

Rosie

Anita

Melissa

Kitty's Friends

chapter 1
William says no!

William woke up feeling . . . different. He looked around. His room was the same – posters on the wall, books on his shelf, and a half-finished model car on the little table. On the pin board were all the postcards his dad had sent from abroad, the latest three from Saudi Arabia, where he was working. It looked so hot there. William listened to the rain on the window, and groaned.

What had changed? He felt as if he'd

turned into a monster overnight, with scales and waving feelers, horns and big, big teeth. He felt as if he could just chew up everything in that room – *chomp, chomp, chomp* through all the furniture, saving the duvet and curtains for pudding.

A silent growl started inside his head and vibrated through his whole body. It said William had had enough.

He heard his mother fill the kettle and call upstairs, 'Hurry up, William!' in a very cheerful voice.

'It's all right for you, Mum,' he muttered. '*You* don't have to go to horrible old school.'

Then he listened as his sister Sally scurried across into the bathroom, singing the latest number one hit. She sounded happy. 'It's all right for you,' he muttered. *Your* friends are always nice to *you*.'

The trouble had started about two weeks ago. It was Kitty's fault. Well, maybe not entirely. Rosie had been just as bad and, although reluctant, Anita went along with the others. No, the real problem was Tim. It was definitely Tim's fault. Sometimes William hated him.

When Tim was a new boy at school nobody liked him very much, and he bullied William – until the great day Kitty stood up to him and everybody was on her side. But after that, Tim said he was sorry, and everybody started to like him – especially the other boys, because he was so good at sport. Now he was really popular.

These days it seemed to William that the others were always talking and laughing about things he didn't quite understand. He was sure they spent a lot of time together without inviting him. Worst of all, Kitty had always been his special friend, since they'd grown up next door to each other – and now it felt as if she had moved away from him, inside her head, in a way he didn't understand. It just wasn't fair.

Kitty had once told him that lots of things aren't fair, but William thought the most unfair thing of all is when your friends seem to like somebody else better. If you're bad at games, and quiet, and not particularly clever or anything . . . well, it's *obviously* unfair. Because you can't change what you're like.

William jumped up, got dressed and looked in the mirror. He wanted to glimpse the monster who growled inside him, because that *would* be a change. But all he saw was the same old face, with freckles, floppy sandy hair and those ears which stuck out just a *little* bit too much to make him happy. He frowned.

He realised what was wrong with his silly face. It was too nice! He pictured Tim's cropped hair, and the look of confidence on his face mixed with a little bit of meanness . . . and knew that *he*, William, looked like somebody who

Kitty's Friends

wouldn't say boo to a goose. Which was true – although since he'd never met a goose he was only guessing.

He remembered how two weeks ago Kitty had said, 'Do you mind if I don't come to your house tonight, William? I mean, I know I promised but . . . oh, you don't mind, do you?' And all William said was, 'That's fine.' Then he saw her running out of the school gate with Rosie and Tim.

Now he packed his books into his school bag, but as he reached across he knocked his model off the table and it fell to bits on the floor. In his head William roared with fury. This was going to be one of those days.

Kitty and friends

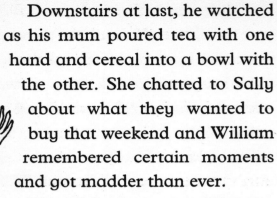

Downstairs at last, he watched as his mum poured tea with one hand and cereal into a bowl with the other. She chatted to Sally about what they wanted to buy that weekend and William remembered certain moments and got madder than ever.

'Can I borrow your crayons, William?' Rosie had asked.

'Yes,' he had said.

'Will you lend me ten pence, William?' pleaded Kitty.

'No problem,' he had replied.

'Oh, William, I can't do these sums. Will you help me?' Anita had whispered.

'OK,' he had answered.

'Hey, William, let's have that library book first, I really want to read it,' demanded Mel.

'Sure,' he had shrugged.

'I'm hungry, William, give us half that chocolate,' Tim had said.

Kitty's Friends

'Oh . . . all right,' William had agreed.

It was like that all the time. They all expected him to be nice to them, because he always was. And the truth was, he really didn't mind. But if you're nice to other people, you sort of expect them to be nice back, don't you? And that wasn't always the case. Sometimes he felt like a very nice, comfortable, familiar old chair that nobody noticed any more.

'They squash me,' he muttered.

'What's that, dear?' asked Mum.

'Um . . . I said I'd like coffee.'

'You never have coffee, Bill!' smiled Mum. 'But eat your toast, love, Kitty'll be here any minute.'

These days Sally walked with Kitty and William along the main road, then left them at the corner of the smaller road their school was in, while she went on a little bit further to big school. Kitty's brother Dan went to a different school, a bus ride away.

'I don't want to walk to school with Kitty,' William growled.

'What?' Mum exclaimed.

'That's silly!' jeered Sally. 'You always . . .'

William banged the table so the plates and mugs jumped. 'I don't ALWAYS anything!' he shouted. 'I want a change!'

'Don't be such a little monster!' yelled Sally.

'This isn't like you, William,' said Mum, looking worried.

The doorbell rang. Without another word William jumped up and pulled on his coat. In that second he decided he wouldn't talk to Kitty today, so that she would soon wonder what was wrong, and ask him. He'd tell her, and she'd be sorry and everything would be like it was before.

The rain danced on the pavement. Sally took her big pink umbrella from the hall stand and said, 'Come on, Kitty, don't get wet.'

Kitty huddled up, but when Sally turned to William and said, 'Come on under here, Squirt – plenty of room for three,' William shook his head. As they walked on, Kitty chatted to Sally about a television programme she'd watched, and didn't even notice William was silent.

When it came to the turning and Sally said goodbye, Kitty grinned at William.

'You look funny, Will – the rain's running down your face and your nose is red. You look like a drowned rat!'

Furious, William frowned, but said nothing. Inside him the monster flashed red eyes and flexed powerful claws.

At that moment Melissa came running up, carrying a blue umbrella. Kitty dived beneath, and the cousins walked a couple of metres ahead of William, all the way into school.

By the time it came to break William felt crosser than ever. He could hardly concentrate on his lessons because he felt so out of sorts. He decided that nobody liked him, and that they never would like him, and so he might as well act like the sort of boy who deserved not to be liked. Instead of saying 'Yes' all the time, so they took him for granted, he would show what sort of bad creature lived inside him. That would teach them!

Kitty's Friends

Rosie bounced up to him with a big grin. 'Hey, William, have one of these,' she said, offering her packet of chocolate biscuits.

'No thanks,' William said coldly, turning away.

Anita was standing nearby and saw what had happened. 'Is something the matter, William?' she asked gently. 'Do you want to come and have a talk?'

'No,' he snapped.

Just then Kitty came up, arm in arm with Melissa. All William could think of was how much Kitty used to dislike her cousin, and moan to him about her. Now they were best friends.

He didn't like that and growled inside.

'Will you do me a favour, Will ...?' Kitty began in her most wheedling voice.

'Of course Will will,' Mel interrupted, laughing.

'No – I won't!' he said.

At that Kitty looked really surprised.

'Don't you want to know what it was?' she asked.

'No.'

William mooched off on his own, and came across Tim, who was standing with two other boys.

'I was just talking about you, Will,' Tim said. 'How'd you like to come skating on Saturday afternoon with us?'

Kitty's Friends

Though he felt a tiny jump for joy at what he heard, William still growled, 'No!'

Then the bell rang, and they all poured back into the classroom. For the rest of the morning William had a tight feeling inside him, as if he had to keep zipped up or else something terrible might come out. Not monster growls this time, but great big, lonely howls. That would be the worst thing in the world.

At the end of the morning Kitty rushed over and took his arm. 'Come with me, William,' she demanded.

'Why?' he began.

'Because I want to talk to you – on your own,' she said, waving the others away.

She turned to face him. 'Come on, Will, what's up? I can see you're upset.'

'No, I'm not.'

'Oh p-lease!' she said. 'Don't tell fibs. You're in a bad mood today, and *you're never* in a bad mood, so something must have happened. Tell me!'

'No.'

'Will, we've been friends since we were little, haven't we?'

'Er . . . yes,' he said reluctantly.

'Well then!'

William looked away. In a very small voice he blurted, 'None of you like me any more.'

'What?'

'You just think I'm some nice little doormat you can all walk on. Well, I'm not, so there!'

Kitty kept silent for so long William had to give in and look at her. She'd put her hands on her hips and was looking at him with such a sad, disbelieving face.

'Do you know what favour I was going to ask you?'

14

Kitty's Friends

'No.'

'Well, I knew Tim was going to ask you to go skating, and you'd be bound to say yes, but I was going to persuade you to come to the panto matinee instead. Mum and Dad got tickets, but Dan's got something on at school – and they're going to take us out for tea in a restaurant afterwards. It'll be great!'

William stared at her. His heart gave a little dance on the spot, but his mind stood still and folded its arms stubbornly.

'I don't think so,' he said flatly.

'*What?*'

'I said, no thanks, Kitty.'

'Oh come on, William! Why?'

In his sternest voice (which wasn't very stern,

although he didn't know that) William said, 'I think it's about time I started doing things . . . uh . . . things *I* want to do.'

'And you don't want to come out and have fun with me?'

'No.'

Kitty looked at him for a long time. William's face flushed bright pink under her gaze. At last she shook her head and said, 'You don't even sound like yourself, Will. What's got into you? Shall I call the others over so we can talk about it?'

'NO!' he shouted, turned on his heel and walked away.

He could feel Kitty's astonished expression following him, so he walked more quickly, because he didn't want it to catch him up. It would be so easy to give in – but then they would go on thinking he was the old William who would put up with anything.

So William went and joined the dinner

Kitty's Friends

queue all on his own. It felt a bit lonely but he knew he had to be strong. Even if it made him miserable.

But of course, it wasn't long before he found himself surrounded by the friends. Rosie, Anita, Melissa, Kitty and Tim were suddenly standing there, quietly and almost shyly, as if they didn't know what to say. That makes a change, he thought, trying not to show he cared.

'All right, Will?' said Tim.

'Can we stand with you?' asked Anita.

'Want a crisp?' offered Rosie.

'You'll really like that book – I'll let you have it now,' Melissa murmured.

'William, I'd really love it if you came out with my family,' pleaded Kitty.

William looked at them all. He knew they knew what was wrong with him, so there wasn't much more to be said. He'd made his point – and after all, they *were* his friends.

With just the faintest hint of a smile he nodded at them all, then he spoke to Kitty.

'Wouldn't you rather take Mel or Rosie?' he asked casually.

'NO, William – I wouldn't! You're my first choice. Don't you get it?'

'Go on, William, you'll have a great time . . . I wish I could go . . . It'll be so cool . . . I heard the panto's brilliant,'

Kitty's Friends

came a babble from the others. They all looked at him expectantly.

'OK, I will then,' he said.

'Oh *thanks*, Will!' Kitty squeaked.

And at that, the cross old monster who had tried its best to take William over gave a last little growl, then went back to sleep. Until the next time he might be needed.

chapter 2
Rosie's big race

It was always the same, Rosie decided.
You thought you were fine about it, just
fine, with no butterflies in your tummy at
all. Who gets nervous? Not Rosie. But then
the day comes and when you wake up it's
more than flutterbies. Much more.

It's as if somebody's grabbed your
stomach and hung it on a line to dry.
Then – *whoosh* – goes the wind, right
through you. And that feels so bad you

can't speak, not with the shivering of it, deep inside your bones.

Rosie loved sport, and went to a junior athletics club meeting every Saturday afternoon. She liked long jump and high jump, and that was because (Kitty said) her legs were so long she didn't need a pole. She enjoyed relay races, hurdles and just about everything. But her favourite thing was running. 'Life's a race, our Rosie,' her dad used to say, and Rosie was determined to *win*. Every time.

Yet today she woke up convinced that she wouldn't. Her club was taking part in a sort of tournament against others from the area, and although Rosie knew it was

all meant to be fun – not like the Olympics or anything that really mattered – she still wanted to do well. Which is to say, she knew that anything less than winning wasn't good enough for her. And that was why she felt so terrible on the morning of her big race.

'Come and eat breakfast, Rosie, I've made you bacon and eggs – and fried bread!' called Mum. 'Don't let it get cold!'

Rosie slowly walked downstairs – into chaos.

It was quite late because everybody had slept in, and now they all wanted breakfast at once. Her family was big, everybody was tall, the kitchen was small, and it didn't work very well! Rosie's three teenage brothers were wandering between the kitchen and the sitting-room, where the television chattered loudly in the corner.

Robbie dropped his toast and roared with fury.

Kitty's Friends

Ben slurped from a big mug of tea.

Sam threw back his dreadlocks to munch on an enormous bacon sandwich.

Then Sara came running downstairs in her dressing-gown, shrieking at the top of her voice that everybody was making too much noise!

All the time Rosie's mum was calmly adding more rashers of bacon to the frying pan, which sizzled and made a delicious smell.

'I'm not hungry, Mum,' Rosie said in a small voice.

'Hey, Robbie, who d'you think'll score today?' called Ben.

'Carter – but I still think he's rubbish!' Robbie replied, giving his brother a playful punch.

'Not as rubbish as you!' came the rude reply.

'Did I tell you we got a gig at Bojangles Club tonight?' said Sam to nobody in particular.

'Mum, you promised you'd help me pay for those shoes,' begged Sara, putting her arms around her mother and getting in the way of the cooking.

'You don't really need them, Sarey,' smiled Mum. 'Here, Rosie – eat up.'

'Come shopping with me, and I bet you like them,' said Sara.

'I don't want breakfast,' whispered Rosie, taking the

plate and turning away.

'OK, then – I'll eat it for you,' said Ben, snatching the plate.

'You coming to meet Dad for a coffee later?' Sam asked his brothers.

'Hmmm, well – just make sure you remind him to pay that bill!' called Mum, with a frown, turning down her mouth at the corners. Ever since Dad moved out she'd been cross whenever the kids saw him.

Nobody bothered with Rosie. She grabbed an apple, flung herself on the settee and tried to see the screen past her brothers, who all lounged around on the floor in front of it. Then Sam picked up his guitar and began to strum over the noise of the television, driving Rosie mad.

In her mind she heard the crack of the starting gun and her stomach turned over. She imagined her legs turning to jelly, and wanted to rush into the kitchen and sit on Mum's knee, like she did when she was a little girl. But she wouldn't. Not with all this noise going on. What did her brothers and sister care? They'd only laugh at her.

They haven't even remembered to wish me luck, thought Rosie miserably. All they care about is themselves.

The minutes dragged. One by one Sam, Ben, Robbie and Sara disappeared, slamming the front door. As if in a dream Rosie heard them calling out their plans to each other, ignoring her, like she didn't exist. She was glad her mum had finally stayed firm about that shopping trip. It wasn't fair if Sara got new shoes when Rosie needed new trainers. Sara got everything – just because she was nearly fourteen and could get her own way by nagging. Poor Mum didn't stand a chance.

Rosie wandered into the kitchen, picked up a tea towel and began to dry the plates.

'Good girl,' said Mum, her arms deep in the washing-up bowl.

Kitty's Friends

'I've got my big race today,' Rosie said after a while, trying to sound casual.

'I know, sweetheart, so I'll drop you off at the sports centre on my way into town.'

Mum emptied the bowl with a big *splosh*.

'Oh,' said Rosie. She felt her spirits swoosh down the pipes with the dirty washing-up water.

A couple of hours later, changed into her running gear and tracksuit, Rosie got into the car. Mum seemed very absent-minded, and hardly said a word on the journey. When they reached the sports centre, Rosie noticed boys and girls she knew, most of them with their dads, talking excitedly as they went into the building. That made her feel even worse – if that were possible.

'Bye, Rosie-Posie – and good luck!' called Mum, with a big grin, as Rosie got out of the car.

'Mum, won't you . . .?' Rosie began.

'What?'

'Oh – nothing.'

She walked inside, passing people she knew, saying hello, *pretending* to be relaxed. Coach Dave patted her on the shoulder and said she'd do well, he knew it. Rosie shook her head, but he'd already rushed off to encourage one of the others, and didn't see.

Suddenly a voice said, 'Hey, Rosie!' She looked around and saw Tim, standing in his tracksuit with his hands on his hips.

'What are you doing here?' asked Rosie.

'I'm running. Just joined the club and

Kitty's Friends

Dave said it would be good practise.'

'You're running against *me*?'

'You and a few others, Rosie! Come to think of it, you might as well all go home!'

Tim folded his arms in that cocky way she both liked and hated. She did the same and tossed her head, saying, 'No chance!'

They heard somebody calling them and walked through to the track. Rosie asked Tim if anybody had come to watch him.

'Mum, of course – couldn't keep her away! But I told her not to embarrass me by yelling too loudly.'

'Oh right,' said Rosie.

Her tummy did that terrible lurch and dip again, making her want to be sick.

Rosie started her warm-up exercises. She

ran up and down on the spot. She banged her arms on her sides, then shook them. She leaned forward from the waist, and stretched first one leg then the other.

'Starting line, guys!' called Coach Dave.

There was a bustle and kerfuffle as twelve children rushed to find their places. Rosie walked more slowly, thinking how odd it was – how you could feel all on your own in a big group of people. But as she thought that, she suddenly felt very strong and determined. Taking a very deep breath, she whispered to herself, 'OK, Rosie, now it's just you against the world.' But it wasn't.

As she stood there, dimly aware of Tim in the next lane but one, she heard a terrific chorus of 'Ros-ie, Ros-ie! Run Rosie run! Ros-ie, Ros-ie! Run Rosie run!'

She looked over to the fence and there they all were in a row:

30

Kitty's Friends

Sam, Ben, Robbie and Sara, all waving, with Mum's face split in the biggest smile ever – and best of all, Dad next to her.

'Rosie's the best! Rosie's the best!' shouted her family.

'Noisy, aren't they?' said the girl next to her in a rather nasty voice. Rosie didn't care. 'Too right!' she replied happily.

Kitty and friends

Suddenly calm, she took a deep breath and tensed, waiting for the signal. When it came she was off like a bullet from a gun. Everything inside her was pushing and pushing, wanting to pass that finishing line first. She could hear the cries of 'Rosie! Come on, Rosie!' above all the names other families and friends called out, and that made her run even faster.

Kitty's Friends

Rosie crossed the finish line. She was sure she'd come first and felt a great firework burst inside her . . . until she saw Coach Dave run over to Tim and clap him on the back.

'Hey, we've got a new star!' he called out.

Seconds later he was at Rosie's side. 'Bad luck, Rosie,' he said sympathetically, 'but there were only seconds in it. We got a first and a second place, so I think you've both done the club proud.'

For a second Rosie wanted to cry because she hadn't won. Then something wonderful happened. When she was practically knocked off her feet by all the wild hugs that arrived in the shape of her family, she realised . . . *she didn't care.*

'You were great, Rosie,' yelled Ben and Robbie together.

'Well done, l'il sis,' whispered Sam.

'He only won 'cos he's a boy!' Sara hissed. 'But still, you ran so fast!'

'You did so well, love!' said Dad, taking her breath away with the strength of his hug.

'We wanted to give you a big surprise,' smiled Mum.

'You did too!' Rosie laughed. 'I thought...'

'I know what you thought,' said Mum. 'Silly Rosie.'

Just then Tim appeared at her side, and she introduced him to everybody.

'No hard feelings?' Tim asked, looking Rosie straight in the eye.

'None at all,' she said, 'but I tell you what, Champ . . .'

'What's that?'

'Next race . . . don't think you'll have it so easy! Better go into training now!'

'That's our girl!' laughed Mum and Sara, punching their fists in the air.

chapter 3
Anita and the attic ghost

Anita's home was in the middle of an old terrace close to the centre of the town. Mr and Mrs Attra had bought it when she was a baby, but now there were three little brothers as well it sometimes felt very small. Mr and Mrs Attra were very busy, and Anita often found herself in charge of her little brothers. Sometimes that made her fed up.

Every now and then she wanted to

Kitty's Friends

shout, 'I don't want to!' or 'It's not fair!' or 'Why me?' or any of the other rebellious phrases she had learnt from her friend Kitty. But there wasn't any point really. Rahul was six, and the twins, Rajesh and Dinesh, four, and they followed Anita around like ducklings. One day she snapped, 'Quack, quack, quack,' at them, flapping her hands like wings – but they just laughed, thinking it was a game, and did the same to her.

'You can *go off* brothers, you know,' she muttered darkly.

'Mum said you've got to play a game with us,' said Rahul in that knowing voice which drove her mad.

All Anita wanted right now was a little time to herself. Kitty had a birthday coming up and she'd decided to make her a special card. But how could she concentrate on that with three little brothers getting in the way? She went to find her mother in the kitchen. Mrs Attra was chopping onions very fast, and the kitchen was full of the spicy smells from her delicious cooking.

'Mum, the boys are getting on my nerves,' she complained, 'and I want to do my own stuff. Can't they watch TV?'

Mrs Attra sighed. 'Daddy doesn't like that, you know. He hates the programmes on now. In any case, he'll be back any minute with two of his friends. There's something important they want to discuss, so they'll be using the sitting-room. Can't you take the boys upstairs and play a game?'

'But Mum, I'm *always* playing with them,' Anita whined.

'And I'm always cooking,' said her mum very quietly. 'I suppose we all have our jobs.'

'But I wanted to . . .' Anita started to protest. Then she stopped, because she noticed how tired her mother looked. Mrs Attra worked hard at home and had a part-time job as well, and always seemed to be making piles of food for them, and for all the family and friends who endlessly came to visit.

'I could cook the meal,' Anita said hopefully.

'I'd much rather you kept your brothers happy,' said Mrs Attra.

Anita felt guilty for moaning, but she also felt rather cross at being made to feel so guilty, and she wondered if she could ever win.

'Be a good, helpful girl now,' said her mother absent-mindedly, as she turned away and began to throw the meat into the frying pan, creating a deafening sizzle.

She had no choice. Anita looked at her brothers, standing in a row in the hall, and she couldn't help scowling. She stalked upstairs without saying anything, and of course they followed her, one by one.

It was getting dark. Rain lashed against the windows. The house was warm and cosy, but a chilly wind blew inside Anita's head. 'Now listen Rahul, and listen Raj and Dinny, I don't think it's fair that I have to look after you. But I'll tell you what we'll do . . .'

'Read a story, Nita – a story!' chorused the little ones.

Anita had planned to make them sit down and do some drawing – although she

knew the little ones would only keep at it for about five minutes before they got bored. But Raj and Dinny had given her an idea. She'd show them!

'Well, I won't read you a story but . . . I'll tell you a made-up one instead,' she said. 'And since I'm bored with kids' stuff, this is going to be a very *scary* story, OK?'

As if on cue the rainstorm rattled the window with a sudden gust, so the three boys squealed with a mixture of excitement and fear and jumped in a heap on Anita's bed.

'Once upon a time, and not so very long ago, there were three little boys who lived alone in a big old house in the middle of a dark, dark forest,' she began. 'And what do you think their names were?'

'Rahul, Rajesh and Dinesh!' said Rahul. 'But there's something wrong.'

'What?' Anita demanded, annoyed.

'Well, real children aren't allowed to live

alone, it's against the law. They have to have a grown-up with them,' Rahul pronounced, in his most 'know-it-all' way.

'Do you want me to tell you this story or not?'

'Yes, yes!' pleaded the twins.

'Well, no more interruptions! As I was saying – there were these three boys called Ay, Bee and Cee, and they lived in a strange country with no laws, where there were no grown-ups, and so they lived all alone in this big dark house, and at night when the wind blew they heard the branches of the trees going *tap, tap, tap* against the windows just as if they were little fingers on the glass. And sometimes the wind sounded like a voice, crying, *"Let me in, let me in"*.'

Rahul was quiet now. Rajesh and Dinesh put their thumbs in their mouths and cuddled close to their older brother, their eyes wide.

'The thing about living by themselves was this – there was nobody to tell them what to do. They could get up when they wanted and go to bed when they wanted. They never had to wash or clean their teeth and they could eat what they liked . . .'

'Where did the food come from,' asked Rahul.

'Magic, of course! It just appeared – that's what happens in stories! What they had to do was leave a list on the kitchen table, and in the morning it was all there . . .'

'I only like Mum's food,' mumbled Dinesh through his thumb.

'Shush!' said Anita sternly. 'Anyway, one day, when it was darker than usual, and the wind was making really *scary* noises all around the house, the boys heard a sound in the distance that made their *blood run cold*.'

Kitty's Friends

'What?' squeaked Rajesh.

'It . . . sounded . . . like . . . er . . . all the monsters and ghosts in the universe rolled into one. It sort of groaned, then it yowled, then it roared. And it was coming nearer, and nearer and –'

'You're frightening the little ones,' gulped Rahul, moving nearer to his brothers, so they were just a tangle of arms and legs on the bed.

Just then Dinesh looked up at the ceiling, an expression of terror on his face.

'Nita – what's that?' he whispered.

'Oh, what now?' asked Anita irritably.

'Shush . . . listen,' hissed Rahul.

'I can *hear* something,' cried Rajesh.

Anita listened. She thought she heard a strange scratching sound above their heads but didn't want it to be true. She froze. But

then the wind sent another handful of rain to rattle like stones on the window, and she breathed a sigh of relief.

'Silly things – it's just the weather!' she jeered.

At that her brothers seemed to relax again, except that Dinesh cast one last fearful look at the ceiling.

'OK, go on with the story,' Rahul demanded.

'I don't feel like it now,' Anita groaned, not liking to admit to them or to herself that she was a *teeny* bit frightened by the atmosphere she'd created with her own words!

At that moment their mother began to call them to come down for some food, and Anita sighed with relief. But she had reckoned without Rahul.

'We want you to finish the story after

we've eaten, don't we?'

The twins – who always agreed with him – nodded.

'I don't want to,' Anita said firmly, folding her arms.

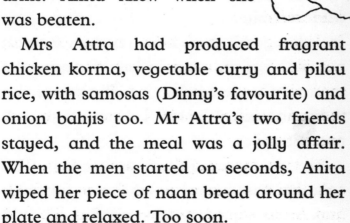

'Well, if you don't I'll tell Mum and Dad you made up a really horrible scary story just to frighten us because you were cross,' replied Rahul, folding his arms. Anita knew when she was beaten.

Mrs Attra had produced fragrant chicken korma, vegetable curry and pilau rice, with samosas (Dinny's favourite) and onion bahjis too. Mr Attra's two friends stayed, and the meal was a jolly affair. When the men started on seconds, Anita wiped her piece of naan bread around her plate and relaxed. Too soon.

Looking as good as gold, Rahul suggested the children went back upstairs.

'You can sit down, Mum, before you put the twins to bed, while Anita finishes the story she was telling us.'

At that the little ones looked both scared and excited at once, but Mrs Attra didn't notice. She reached out to smooth Anita's hair and said she was a good girl.

Who'd have horrible little brothers? thought Anita, but knew she had no choice. So she led the way upstairs.

'This time we'll go into *your* room,' she said, stopping herself from glancing up at the ceiling. All three boys piled on Rahul's bed – the twins slept in bunks across the room. Anita decided that if she was going to have to finish the story she might as well make it good.

'Go on, then,' Rahul demanded. 'You were at the bit when the monster was making noises and getting nearer . . .'

'Yes, well it did. And the boys, Ay, Bee and Cee, wondered what to do. The night before they'd found this very old roll of paper in a box covered in spider webs, all long and sticky . . .'

'Ugh,' said Dinesh.

'. . . and the parchment – that's what it was, a parchment – said they would only escape from the haunted magic house if –'

'I thought they liked it, 'cos they could eat and do anything!' Rahul interrupted.

'Be quiet!' Anita snapped. 'The thing was, *despite* that, they knew there was a big world out there and they wanted to be free. So this parchment said that one of them had to go outside and face up to the creature and –'

'Kill it!' squealed Rajesh.

'No . . . er . . . be tested as to what makes a very brave person, tho' they wouldn't know what the special test was until they came to face with those *horrible* eyes glowing in the darkness, and saw the *dripping* mouth . . .'

Dinesh and Rajesh started to giggle nervously, but Rahul held up his hand.

'Shh – what's that noise?' he whispered. The children froze.

The wind had dropped by now, so it was easy to hear. Four pairs of eyes were slowly raised to the ceiling, where the noise came from.

Scratch, scratch, scratch.

'What is it?' breathed Dinesh.

'Must be a mouse,' said Anita.

Scratch, scratch, scratch.

'Too big for a mouse,' murmured Rahul.

'I don't like it, Anita,' Rajesh said softly, clutching his sister's hand.

Anita didn't like it either, but she couldn't show she was nervous. The obvious thing would have been to run downstairs and fetch Mum and Dad, but she dreaded the teasing she knew Dad's friends would dish out. She also worried that she might get into trouble for scaring her little brothers – especially the twins. She could see tears in their eyes . . .

'I know – this is the test!' she said in a bright voice. 'We have to find out what's making the strange noise, and rescue it!'

Scratch, scratch, scratch.

'I think it's a real *ghost*,' whispered Rahul helpfully.

Anita took a deep breath, knowing she couldn't delay any longer or the little ones would wail and Rahul would rush downstairs and tell Mum. So she jumped up and went out to the landing where the aluminium loft ladder was tucked back against the wall. She'd seen Dad go up into the attic. All you had to do was pull out the ladder until it clicked, then climb up, push the trapdoor open, reach for the light switch on the left and there you were . . . *Help*! she thought, not wanting to do it at all.

The scratching seemed to grow louder

– much too strong for a mouse or a bird. It seemed to be everywhere now. Her brothers' eyes were as wide as saucers. She knew she had to solve the mystery.

Within seconds she was at the top of the ladder pushing at the trapdoor. It moved to one side easily. The blackness in the attic was so thick she could almost feel it and, as she reached for the switch, the musty, dusty air caught in her nostrils.

Her heart was thumping as she felt around in the darkness, hoping her fingers wouldn't meet something horrible . . . like the milky, misty, chilly fingers of . . . something that wasn't real.

It was then that she saw two eyes staring at her, gleaming like marbles in the darkness.

'Oh!' she cried in fear.

'What ?' hissed the three little boys from below. *Click*! went the switch, flooding the roof space with yellow light.

Then Anita started to laugh. Relief and delight poured down from above and wrapped around Rahul, Rajesh and Dinesh like a silvery cloak. She beamed over her shoulder – 'We've got a visitor, boys!' – then clambered up into the attic and disappeared.

Within minutes she was back again, carrying something. The boys saw her carefully tuck whatever it was inside her top so she could climb down, then there she was in front of them.

'Look!'

Peeping out was a little stripey face, with two ears, a greyish-pink nose, two yellow eyes and a splendid set of whiskers.

'It's a kitten!' squealed the boys in unison.

They went downstairs. Mr Attra's friends had just left, and the parents were washing the dishes in the

Kitty's Friends

kitchen. They gaped when they saw the visitor. Then came the deafening chorus.

'Oh please, can we keep it . . .'

'It's only little . . .'

'We want a pet!'

'He wants to live with us, that's why he came!'

Mum dried her hands and Dad put down the tea towel, and they all trooped through to the living-room, Anita carrying the kitten like a trophy. The little creature snuggled up to her as if – yes – this was meant to be.

She told her parents everything that had happened – except for the fact that it was a scary story. And for once Rahul kept quiet.

'The cat must have come through from one of the other houses in the row,' said Dad. 'All the attics are joined, and with houses this old there are bound to be little gaps.'

Kitty and friends

'We'll have to give it back,' said Mum.

The children all groaned, and Dinny's mouth began to wobble. Seeing their faces, Dad said he'd go and knock on every door and try to find out who owned the kitten. In the meantime Mrs Attra fetched a saucer of milk and the kitten lapped it up, purring like a miniature engine.

It wasn't long before a beaming father strode back into the room. 'Guess what?' he said. 'The people at number six – oh, they're really nice, my love, and they've invited us to go along for tea. How come we've never met them?'

'*So what did they say?*' Anita interrupted.

'Yes, well, their cat had a litter of kittens and they managed to find homes for them all except this one. So they were planning to take her – she's a little girl, by the way – to the rescue home tomorrow, because they can't manage two cats. Yesterday Mr Owen was putting away a box in his attic and they reckon the little thing must have followed him up there, somehow.'

'She heard them talking about the home and ran away to *us*,' said Anita.

'Yes, yes – can we keep her? Please, Mum, please, Dad!' cried the boys, until Dad put his fingers in his ears.

'What do you say, Mummy?' he grinned.

'Well . . . it's only a very small mouth to feed,' she replied, with a big smile.

When the noise died down at last, and Mum took the twins upstairs to bed, Rahul and Anita sat quietly, listening to the kitten's loud, contented purr.

'You passed the test, Nita,' said Rahul.

'What test?' she asked.

'Have you forgotten your story? The bravery test of course! And because of that – well – I think you should be allowed to choose her name.'

'Thanks, little brother – and now you mention it, I've already decided.'

'What?'

'Lakshmi!'

'Who . . .?'

'Don't you remember all our special stories – the ones Dad told us about all the gods and goddesses? Lakshmi is the goddess of riches and gifts and things like that.'

'Brilliant!' her brother said, "cos she's the best present we'll have this year!'

chapter 4
Tim's elephant

'Sometimes you just have to have a clear-out,' said Mum, banging about the flat in that way Tim hated.

It told him she was busy.

It told him there would be trouble.

It made him want to run for cover.

Mum had been getting crosser and crosser that their new home was already a mess. She couldn't cope with it.

'If you live in a small place you just have to throw things away,' she said.

There were black bin-bags in the hall, filled with old magazines, broken toys, used wrapping paper, empty boxes she had been keeping in case they came in handy . . . all sorts of things. Next to them was a pile of old clothes for the charity shop, and a box of china and other bits and pieces for the church jumble sale.

All this sweeping up and clearing out made Tim feel a little sad – as if Mum was rooting out their past and giving it away. And Tim thought the past didn't belong in bin-bags – thrown out and forgotten. It belonged in his memory, where he could keep it warm.

But the trouble was, now Dad wasn't around any more, Mum said she had to 'move on'. She was much happier than she had been and Tim was glad of that. He knew all this briskness and busyness was her way of showing she was fine. His way was . . . oh, but he knew he *wasn't* fine.

That was why he was sometimes cross in school, and tried to act so tough all the time.

Mum had a glint in her eye. She turned to Tim and clapped her hands. 'Now let's start on *your* room!' she said.

They went along the hall and pushed open the door. Tim's heart dropped to the floor when he saw, as if for the first time, how untidy his room was. He knew what Mum would say before she said it. 'Lots for us to clear up in here!' Oh no! he thought. Mum tripped over his skateboard and muttered something cross under her breath. Oh double-power no! he thought.

Mum put a box on the floor for the toys she said Tim didn't need any more.

'But what if I want them?' he mumbled.

'WANT doesn't mean NEED,' said

Mum briskly. 'Think of it this way – if you give things away to the charity jumble sale, you'll be helping other people. It's a good cause. Now – look at *this* old thing! You've grown out of it, but some little child might like it.' Swooping down, she picked up Tim's old toy elephant.

Tim liked sports and skateboarding and watching TV. Because he was tall he looked older than the other kids in his class, and felt quite grown-up now he had to look after Mum. Big boys don't take soft toys to bed, of course . . . but that doesn't stop you liking your old favourites. And so he kept old Effie the Elephant on the little chair in the corner of his bedroom, where he could see her. When his friends came round he was careful to hide her in the cupboard, in case he got teased. But he liked Effie very much – even though she was a dirty beige colour now, with an ear that was half hanging off and one

embroidered eye all unravelled. Her trunk was wonky and the stuffing had gone funny in one of her legs so it was all lumpy. The truth was, she didn't look much like the soft, cream, cuddly toy Dad had brought home one day when Tim was two years old.

Tim looked at his elephant and saw how ugly she was. Mum popped Effie in the box. 'But *Mum* . . .' Tim began, and then he stopped.

'You're not going to tell me you still play with that old heffalump, are you, love?' smiled Mum.

Tim went red. 'As if!' he said, shuffling his trainers.

For a second he thought the toy was looking at him over the rim of the box, her one good eye very bright. But that couldn't be true, because she wasn't real.

'OK,' said Mum, 'so we'll give it away to a good cause, and make more room for your new things.'

Not long after that, Mum said she'd finished. She made lots of journeys down the stairs to her car, carrying boxes and bags. Tim didn't help her. He wouldn't even watch, as bits of their life disappeared into the car, never to be seen again.

Soon the hall was empty. 'There!' said Mum, rubbing her hands together briskly.

Kitty's Friends

'Isn't that better? The whole flat feels bigger now, doesn't it, love?' It was true. Mum flopped down onto the sofa with a cup of tea, and they watched TV together.

That night Tim couldn't sleep. The little chair in his room was empty, and his eyes kept being drawn back to it, even though he tried to stop them. He wondered where Effie was and what she was thinking. But that was silly. He *knew* that. Old toys don't *think* anything. If the old elephant was in a dark, chilly place somewhere, waiting in the box for the jumble sale, she didn't *know* it was dark and chilly, did she? So it didn't matter. Tim got out of bed and put his big plastic spaceman on the chair. But it didn't feel the same.

A few days passed, and Tim missed his elephant. But because he felt a bit silly, he didn't say anything to Mum. She was so pleased that their tiny flat was tidy now, he didn't want to upset her. He knew she wouldn't have made him give Effie away if she had known the truth. Mum just got too enthusiastic sometimes, and didn't stop to think.

Grown-ups are all like that, Tim thought. They just want to *bustle* you, and bounce you into things. They want to make you grow up just like them. But sometimes you don't want to.

He decided he had to be sensible about Effie, and forget her. But when he saw the poster for the Grand Jumble Sale at the church hall he couldn't resist.

'Hey, Mum – why don't we go?' he said.

'No way!' said Mum. 'We don't want to buy any of that old rubbish. We just cleared out!'

'Ah, but you have to pay to get in, and

you can buy coffee and cake, and talk to people,' Tim said, thinking fast. '*You* said it's a good cause, so we should support it.'

Mum nodded thoughtfully. 'You're right,' she said. 'We'll go!'

On Saturday they walked to the church hall, and paid their money to get in. The room was already full of people, pushing and shoving as they tried to get near the stalls. Tim saw an old lady trying on Mum's old red jacket. On another stall he noticed the orange glass vase and the mustard-coloured plates she'd always hated.

Mum saw one of her friends and went off to join the queue for coffee. Tim told her he would come to find her a bit later, and started to walk slowly round the hall, looking for the toy stall.

It wasn't that he planned to buy his elephant back, because he knew that would be very babyish. And in any case, he didn't have any money. It was just that he

wanted to see who got her, so he'd be able
to imagine her in her new home. He looked
and looked, but when at last he found the
toy stall, he couldn't see Effie at all, and
wondered if she had already been sold.
There were jigsaws, toy cars, wooden trains,
dolls, bats and balls. But no elephant.

Then Tim heard the lady on the stall
say to her friend, 'Wasn't there another
box of toys somewhere?'

'Oh yes, it's under the table,' she replied.
'But it's really old things nobody could
possibly want.'

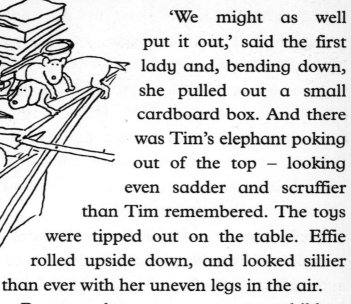

'We might as well put it out,' said the first lady and, bending down, she pulled out a small cardboard box. And there was Tim's elephant poking out of the top – looking even sadder and scruffier than Tim remembered. The toys were tipped out on the table. Effie rolled upside down, and looked sillier than ever with her uneven legs in the air.

By now there were so many children crowding round Tim could hardly see. They held out their coins and grabbed the toys, choosing all the newest-looking ones first – of course. Nobody bothered to pick Effie up. Tim had to admit to himself that his elephant was the least attractive toy on the stall.

That was why he was pleased when at last a little girl turned Effie over in her hands.

'Look, Mum – it's an elephant,' she said.

'Ugh, it's a dirty old reject,' shuddered her mother, and pulled the child away.

Then a mean-looking small boy jabbed Effie with his finger. 'How much is this then?' he asked the lady on the stall.

'Oh . . . er . . . twenty pence,' she said. Tim held his breath, hoping the boy wouldn't buy his old elephant.

'Nah – too much for that old thing,' he said at last, chucking Effie down on her head.

Kitty's Friends

At that moment a familiar voice said, 'Hi, Tim.' He turned around, and there was Kitty, grinning at him. 'I wouldn't expect to meet you at a jumble sale!'

'Oh, Mum made me come,' he mumbled. 'I just want to get home and watch the football.'

'Don't blame you,' Kitty laughed. 'I've come with Dan 'cos he likes buying old books. Now, what've we got here?' She picked up a jigsaw, and put it down. She looked at a plastic shuttlecock set, and flicked through the pages of a big storybook. Then she fingered a necklace of pink beads. At last she picked up Effie.

'Oh you poor little elephant,' Kitty said softly. Effie stared back at her through her one good eye. *Oh please buy Effie*, thought Tim, because he knew Kitty was kind, even though (like him) she seemed cheeky and naughty sometimes.

'You going to buy that?' he asked gruffly.

'Well, the trouble is, I've got lots of soft toys and Mr Tubs is my favourite . . . so I don't think so,' Kitty said. 'But I always feel sad when I see a toy nobody wants, don't you?'

'Not really,' Tim fibbed.

'Anyway, why are you standing here? Are you going to buy something?' Kitty asked.

'Nah,' Tim shrugged. Then Kitty said goodbye and walked away.

Tim waited and waited by the stall. Not so many children were bothering to look now, because most of the toys had been sold. A couple of old ladies came over and looked at what was left.

There was a jigsaw with some pieces missing, a wooden train without its funnel, a furry parrot on a swing that used to make a squawky noise, and a cowboy holster without the guns. And Effie, with her one ear, wonky trunk and damaged eye. She looked sadder than ever as even the old ladies moved away.

Tim noticed that everything left on the stall was missing a part of itself. He realised another thing as well. *He* was missing something. He was missing his elephant. She was part of him – this dirty old toy which had only got so scruffy because she had shared so many games, and been loved so much. Tim smiled to himself as he remembered sending her down a slide into a bowl of water, over and over again. Then hanging her by her ears to dry. Poor Effie!

Just then one of the ladies on the stall picked the elephant up by her trunk. 'Look at this pathetic old thing,' she smiled. 'Jumbo the unwanted jumble!' And the other lady laughed at her joke.

Kitty and friends

That did it. Tim went very red and stepped forward. 'She's not called Jumbo, she's called Effie!' he shouted. 'And she's *mine*. I want to buy her back, please.'

The two ladies were quite taken aback. 'All right, love,' said one. 'It was twenty, but you can have it for ten.'

At that Tim went even redder as he remembered the truth. He rummaged in his pockets, then looked up helplessly. At that moment a hand stretched out from behind him, offering a ten pence coin. He looked round and there was Kitty.

Kitty's Friends

'I think that elephant's sweet,' she said, looking straight into his eyes as if she *knew*. Then another hand came forward, offering twenty pence as a voice said, 'That's really kind of you, Kitty, but you keep your money.' Tim looked up, and there was his mum, smiling at him.

'Do you want to buy that nice old elephant?' she whispered. Tim nodded, unable to speak.

'Well, since it's for a good cause we might as well give the proper price,' said Mum. 'Don't you think that's fair? I expect you think she's worth it, too.' Tim nodded again, as Kitty said, 'Oh, that's for sure! Well, I'd better go and find my brother. Bye, Tim! Bye, Mrs Eaves!'

Tim reached forward to rescue Effie from the stall. As he held her he smelt her furry material and remembered lots of hugs on all those nights when he was very small.

Suddenly he noticed some boys from his class standing by the door. Mum followed his gaze and said in a loud voice. 'That elephant will be lovely for your little cousin, Tim. Here – let's put it in my shopping bag.'

And so Effie was stashed safely away. They walked along the road in silence. Then at last Tim said, 'Thanks, Mum.'

'That's all right, pet,' she replied. 'In any case, it's me who needs to thank you.'

'Why?' Tim asked.

Kitty's Friends

'Because I forgot about Effie,' she said. Tim was puzzled. 'What do you mean?' he asked.

'I was so keen on clearing out I forgot how much you used to love her,' said Mum. 'And I was wrong. So I'm glad you made me remember there should be room in every house for old things with special memories.'

Happily Tim pulled his elephant from the bag, not caring who saw. He looked at her, all funny and squashed, and could have sworn there was a little smile on her face.

'Effie knows that's true, Mum,' he said. 'And you know why? Because elephants *never* forget!'

chapter 5
Who is Melissa?

Once upon a time, Mel thought, there was only one Melissa, and that made things as easy as . . . well, a fairy story. Melissa was her mother and father's sweet little princess, who wore pretty clothes (as princesses must) and was always, always good. But one day Melissa felt as if she were imprisoned in a tower and longed to break free. So she climbed down into the real world, cut off her golden curls, made

Kitty's Friends

all her pretty clothes dirty, called herself
Mel – and lived *normally* ever after.

But of course, it wasn't quite that simple.
Inside Mel there was still Melissa, and
Melissa knew that the clothes Mel wore
didn't always suit what she felt like. Now she
was off on a shopping expedition with her
mum, she knew it could get more confusing
than ever. They'd decided she would have
some new clothes for her birthday, and
Mum was really looking forward to their
morning together. The trouble was, Mel
wasn't at all sure what – or who – she
wanted to look like. How do you know, she
thought, which is the *real* you?

When she took the advice of Kitty's Mr Tubs and became more like Kitty and the other girls, wearing jeans, trainers and fleece tops instead of those fancy dresses, she felt much happier. But she still went to her ballet class, and there it was a different world. Her ballet friends, Chloe and Lisa, read the kind of magazines Kitty scorned, talked about clothes and make-up, and wore sparkly tops and shoes with little heels. They had their ears pierced and were altogether the kind of *girly* girls Kitty and Rosie looked down on.

Of course the truth was, Chloe and Lisa looked down on girls like Kitty and Rosie just as much, and although Mel thought they were *all* being unfair she said nothing. Sometimes it felt very confusing.

It was a beautiful Saturday morning, with fluffy white clouds dotting the blue sky. Mel tucked her arm in her mum's, and they walked briskly, talking about everything under the sun. They headed for the town's brand new shopping mall, where sooner or later you met everybody you knew.

'What do you think you want most?' asked Mum.

'I don't know.'

'You must have some idea! What about a velour tracksuit?'

'Why?'

'I saw a picture of Madonna in one. Sporty *and* fashionable, dear!'

'Mmmm,' said Mel dubiously.

'Or a new jacket . . .?'

'Maybe . . .'

'I wished you'd, well, dressed up a bit more to come out shopping, darling,' sighed Mum. 'How come you always want to wear those jeans?'

Mel was saved from having to reply, because just then a voice called their names. They stopped and waited for Kitty and her mum to catch up. The two mums were sisters and always had a lot to say to each other, so Kitty and Mel moved away to talk to themselves. Kitty seemed to be in a bad mood, so when Mel explained the point of this outing, she just grunted contemptuously.

'Huh – shopping!'

'What about it?'

'It's just about the most boring thing in the world – unless it's for something interesting like toys or games or books.'

'I *like* shopping for clothes,' said Mel, defensively.

'Why?'

Kitty's Friends

'Because . . . er . . . because we all need clothes!'

'Ha, but needing isn't the same as liking,' said Kitty, folding her arms as if there was nothing more to be said.

When the two mothers had finished chatting they headed off in opposite directions, Kitty having refused her mother's suggestion that they accompany Mel and Auntie Susan on the shopping trip. Phew, thought Melissa. She'd imagined Kitty's face as she tried things on, and it wasn't a happy thought.

They were at the entrance to the shopping mall when somebody called out, 'Melissa!' She turned to see Lisa and Chloe walking arm in arm towards them. Her two ballet friends both had long, fringed, dark hair, but Chloe's fell in a sleek curtain to her shoulders, while Lisa's was twisted on top of her head and held in place by two pink clips. The girls were

wearing identical dark pink fleeces, over
little navy denim skirts, with pink tights
and shiny black shoes with chunky heels.

'Oh, girls – you look just like pretty
twins,' cooed Mel's mother.

Unlike Kitty, Chloe and Lisa were
desperate to come along too. Strangely,
Melissa didn't really want them to. Kitty
was sulky and thought everybody should
be a tomboy like her. Chloe and Lisa

Kitty's Friends

were much too clothes-mad and Mel knew they would like whatever her mother liked, and drive her along in the same direction. It was like standing on a crossroads and looking up at a signpost which said, 'Melissa' in one direction and 'Mel' in the other. How was she to know which way to go? How was she to know who she was?

Once you enter a shopping mall you have to forget about the blue sky, the fluffy clouds and the sunlight, and give yourself over to rows of shops, loud music, and the hubbub of footsteps and people talking and laughing, whilst bored babies cry desperately from their pushchairs that they really *hate* shopping. That is what *Waaaa, waaaa, waaa!* means.

A part of Mel wanted to turn around and go home, but she didn't want to hurt her mother's feelings, so turned her mouth up in a smile. Chloe and Lisa were chattering excitedly, and dived into the first shop – a large, very stylish one called Starstruck, leaving Mel and her mother no choice but to follow.

Within minutes the girls were pushing various garments at Mel – who was starting to feel more and more like Melissa. It wasn't because that's what her ballet friends called her; it was because they brought her the kinds of clothes she always used to love.

'Try this!' said Chloe. It was a short-sleeved, close-fitting mini-dress in pink and white stripes with a rose embroidered on the front, picked out in silvery beads.

'This is so lovely!' said Lisa. It was a cropped, white, fake-fur jacket.

'Oh, sweetheart, you'd look so pretty in that outfit,' sighed Mum. 'Go into the changing-room, and then come out and show us.'

Kitty's Friends

'Wait a minute, you haven't got the right shoes,' said Chloe, looking down critically at Melissa's trainers.

'Got to have decent accessories,' Lisa pronounced, and dived off across the shop. She came back in a few minutes with a pair of beaded Chinese mules, and a pale blue denim floppy hat, embroidered on one side with a butterfly. 'Try these for now,' she ordered.

'She'd need some little kitten-heeled boots, Mrs Rawlins,' said Chloe, and Melissa's mum nodded enthusiastically.

'We'll go to the shoe shop next,' she said.

Melissa took the clothes and went into the changing-room, feeling quite excited despite her worry. It didn't take long to get dressed, and when she looked in the mirror she liked what she saw. She felt glamorous,

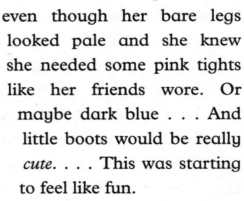

even though her bare legs looked pale and she knew she needed some pink tights like her friends wore. Or maybe dark blue . . . And little boots would be really *cute*. . . . This was starting to feel like fun.

Wearing the dress, the jacket, the hat and the mules (which were wrong but looked better than trainers) she was greeted by cries of enthusiasm. Her mother beamed, while Lisa and Chloe nodded their approval.

'What do you think?' asked Mum.

'I . . . like the dress. But do you think the jacket's a bit . . . over the top?' murmured Mel.

'You look really lovely. Go and look in that long mirror near the door,' said Mum.

Melissa surveyed herself in the mirror. She liked the way she looked, although right at the back of her mind a small voice told her that Kitty would laugh at her in these clothes. Oh, so what? she said to herself, *she* doesn't know anything! She usually looks like a scarecrow!

At that moment she heard a tap on the shop window. She looked up – to her horror William and Tim were outside, watching her! The door was wide open; she couldn't stop them standing there and laughing at her. Because that was what they did.

She wanted the shop floor to turn into a swimming-pool so she could dive down and not be seen.

'Hey, Mel,' called Tim with a mocking smile, 'I didn't know you turned into a Barbie doll on Saturdays.'

'No, that's not it,' said William. 'If you'd known Mel as long as I have, you'd know it's just a case of the old Melissa making a comeback.'

Kitty's Friends

'Oh shut up, William,' said Mel, furiously.

The truth was, she didn't care much what William thought. But she really liked Tim and couldn't bear him to laugh at her. It made her want to cry – but of course she wouldn't show that for the world.

Her face as pink as the dress, she turned on her heels and went back to where the others were waiting.

'Well, what do you think, love?' asked Mum.

'I hate these clothes,' she snapped, and disappeared into the changing-room without another word.

When she came out she handed the discarded clothes to Lisa and Chloe, smiled sweetly at them and whispered, 'Do me a favour and put these back. And hey, look – Mum wanted us to be on our own really, it's supposed to be special, so do you mind if . . .'

'Oh, my mum likes that mother-daughter thing too,' nodded Chloe in a grown-up, understanding way.

'See you at ballet at four,' added Lisa. 'You can tell us what you bought.'

So Mel got rid of her well-meaning friends, and led her surprised mother out of Starstruck. She was relieved to see no sign of the boys because she'd had enough teasing for one day. She thought of suggesting to her mother that they went home, but knew that would be giving in. To what? To the knowledge that she hadn't a clue what she wanted, or rather – *who* she wanted to be. Surely there must be an answer!

She followed her mum around, trying hard to be enthusiastic, but the boys' mockery had certainly taken the gloss off the day. A Barbie doll, indeed! It so happened that Melissa used to love playing with her two Barbies, and there

Kitty's Friends

was nothing wrong with that. After all, people liked different things, and Mum always said that that made the world an interesting place. But Mel knew she didn't want to look like a doll. It was true that a lot of the clothes she saw were much too tight and shiny and self-conscious.

'Oh, look, pet!' Mum cried out, stopping suddenly by one of the newest shops. 'I really like *that*! Why don't we go and try it on?' Mel was just about to say no and turn away, when – in a moment of inspiration – she saw that good old mum might just be right after all . . .

Kitty and friends

* * *

'*A velour tracksuit?*' said Kitty on the phone. 'What on earth's that? Sounds a bit sporty for you, Mel.'

'Just wait and see,' said Melissa. 'We're coming round to yours after my ballet lesson.'

The new outfit got the Chloe and Lisa seal of approval, and when they knocked on Kitty's door, Mel felt sure her cousin would have to say nice things too. And she did.

'Wow, Mel, you look great!' Kitty said, pulling her cousin into the house.

Melissa's birthday tracksuit was made of dark turquoise velvety material with no hood and two white stripes running down the sleeves and the legs. The bottoms were quite wide, and trimmed with three silver zips, with two more closing the jacket pockets. The zips had little chunks of silver hanging from them. Underneath Mel wore a simple black long-sleeved T-shirt with the word COOL in small silver print on the

94

Kitty's Friends

front. The new trainers were white with dark turquoise and silver flashes on the sides.

Daniel came downstairs and shared Kitty's verdict. The two mums murmured together how hard it is to please girls, while the two dads winked at each other and said that was all a lot of nonsense. They were all sitting down to birthday cake and tea when the doorbell rang.

'I asked William and Tim to call in for a piece of cake,' Kitty explained, jumping up.

Mel followed her to the front door, feeling strangely anxious. Why should it matter what your friends thought? she wondered. But it did.

Once they were in the hall the two boys

glanced casually at Mel, then spoke at once.

'That's better, Melissa!' said William.

'Cool, Mel!' said Tim. Disguising her pleasure, Mel shrugged, lounged in the doorway – and put on a fake-serious grown-up voice. 'Looking good is just a question of knowing exactly who you are,' she said.

'*And* who you're not!' said Kitty.

chapter 6
A little magic

There are some times when everything seems dead, when not much is happening, and everybody feels tired and low. February is one of those months, when Christmas has passed and it feels like a very long time until the summer holidays. One cold Monday morning Kitty and her friends clustered together in a corner of the school hall and shared their moans.

'Too much work in school,' said Tim. 'I can't keep up.'

Kitty and friends

'Every time my Dad comes round, Mum yells at him,' said Rosie. 'I hate it.'

'It's ages till my birthday,' said Anita, 'and look at this weather!'

'My sister's always in a bad mood,' said William.

'Mum said I can't have a pocket money rise – so mean!' said Melissa. Kitty said nothing.

Kitty's Friends

They all looked at her expectantly. But she just looked at the ground, scowled, and still didn't speak.

'What about you, Kit?' William asked.

'Hmph . . . just about everything,' she said, and quickly walked away.

'What's wrong with her?' asked Tim. William looked at Melissa. 'Is it what I'm thinking?' he asked.

Kitty's cousin nodded. 'You know our grandma died not very long ago?' she explained. 'Well, you know Kit's mum and my mum are sisters, OK? But Kitty's family always saw more of Gran than we did 'cos we lived further away for so long. Now . . . well, we think she's just missing Gran a lot, that's all. More than any of us, even though we all loved her.'

'Oh,' said Tim, looking awkward.

There was a short silence. Then Rosie's face lit up. 'I've got a brilliant idea!' she said. 'What we need is some magic!'

'*Magic*?' they chorused.

'Yes, magic! Everybody needs a little magic! We're all feeling down, and Kit's the worst, and so we need to cast a spell to make things better. And have some fun!'

'Sounds a good idea,' said William.

'A party!' shouted Anita, clapping her hands.

'A magic party!' cried Mel.

'Fancy dress!' laughed Rosie, giving Tim a light punch on the arm when she saw his face fall. 'Is that a good idea, or what?'

'Oh, I suppose so,' said Tim.

They went into a huddle and made their plans. William said he thought his mum would agree for the party to be at his house, because they had quite a big living-room. They'd all provide some food and drink, and they'd play some of the games they had loved when they were younger.

Kitty's Friends

As for the dressing-up part, Rosie had it all worked out.

'We have to come as somebody sort of make-believe or magical,' she said. 'And nobody's allowed to use a bought costume. Your outfit has to be from stuff at home, like . . .'

'Black bin-bags,' said William.

'Kitchen foil and clingfilm,' said Anita.

'Wire coat-hangers,' said Tim.

'Cardboard and newspaper,' said Rosie.

'Yes, and obviously we can use glue and sticky tape and string, and any colouring stuff,' added Melissa.

'Brilliant!' they all laughed, feeling very excited.

When Kitty wandered back in time for the afternoon lessons, they told her what they had decided and her face lit up, too.

'Just what I need!' she said.

'See? The magic's already starting,' whispered Rosie to Mel. They decided on the following Saturday, as long as William's mum agreed. She did – of course. His sister Sally even said she would help, and William realised that she really liked the idea of joining in, even if she pretended to be grown-up.

Everybody made a list of who would provide what for the party, because it would be so boring if everybody bought crisps and there was nothing else. They also made it a rule that each person had to think of something to do – a game, or some activity – to make the party go with a swing. And of course, there were the costumes to think about and make . . . The week passed very quickly indeed.

When Saturday came, William and Sally decorated the sitting-room with tinsel from the Christmas box that wasn't long put away. It was amazing how shimmering silver draped here and there immediately transformed the room. William's mum put

candles out as well, saying she'd light them
when the guests arrived. Sally stuck joss-
sticks in a flowerpot, which started to send
ribbons of scented smoke up to the ceiling.
Gradually, as it grew dark outside and the
time drew near, the whole house began to
feel special.

At the last minute William rushed

upstairs to transform himself into a wizard. He wore a black top and jeans, which was easy enough, but he'd created a long cloak with a stand-up collar out of shiny bin-liners, with silver stars cut from kitchen foil, stuck all over it. From cardboard he'd made himself a pointed wizard's hat, painted it black and stuck stars all over that as well. His wand was a length of garden bamboo with a cardboard star on the end, all covered in silver. He felt very pleased with his outfit.

The doorbell rang, and on the doorstep stood . . . a vampire. William caught his breath for a split second, so terrifying was the chalky white face, dark hair slicked

Kitty's Friends

back with gel, black-rimmed eyes, and a sinister trickle of red from the corner of the fanged mouth. Then he started to giggle.

'You look brilliant, Tim!'

Tim stepped into the hall, rustling in more shiny black bin-liners, which made a tunic as well as a long plain cloak, over black jeans. He confessed his mum had helped with his make-up, taking special care painting the fangs at the corners of his mouth. 'I had some plastic ones out of a cracker but I couldn't wear them all night!' Tim explained.

Next Rosie and Anita arrived together, both dressed as witches, as William had guessed. Ever-useful bin bags made their dresses and cloaks and, like William, they'd made pointed hats out of cardboard, the brims stuck on with sticky tape. Underneath the hats they'd glued a mixture of string and wool to hang down as witch's hair, and each carried an ordinary kitchen brush to represent a broomstick. Rosie hung plastic spiders from the little gold hoops in her ears, and

Kitty's Friends

Anita carried a stuffed toy black cat – because, she said, Lakshmi might be frightened by them all, and in any case she was the wrong colour.

William was wondering where Kitty was (after all, she only lived next door) when the doorbell rang again. But this time it was Melissa, all dressed up as a fairy. She looked very graceful in a frothy white dress left over from her ballet classes, which she'd decorated with silver foil stars, each one carefully sewn with a stitch in the middle. She wore a silver headdress and some gauzy fairy wings her mother had given her one Christmas. Secretly Rosie thought she should have made her costume, like the rest of them, but on the other hand, the rule was to use things you already had at home, and she had done that.

'Now we've got one *good* magical person,' said Tim.

'Oh, I'm a good wizard!' said William.

Kitty and friends

'And witches can be good!' said Anita indignantly.

'Well, I'm pure *baaaaad*,' growled Tim, and chased them all into the sitting-room.

The children exclaimed over the low lights, silvery decorations, flickering candles and lovely scents. They helped Sally put the food they'd brought on to plates, so there was a fine spread – sandwiches, crisps and snacks, slices of pizza, chicken legs, samosas, sausages, chocolate biscuits, and the delicious, sticky Indian sweets that were Mrs Attra's speciality. William's mum provided soft drinks, and it was all the children could do to stop themselves from eating there and then.

'Games first,' said Rosie in her bossiest voice.

'No, we have to wait for Kitty,' said William.

'Where *is* she?' asked Tim impatiently.

As if on cue the doorbell rang. They all stepped back in surprise when Kitty walked in. Well, actually, she didn't walk, she shuffled. They looked her up and down and couldn't understand what they saw. Kitty was wearing two bin-liners taped together, so they encased her whole body like a sausage skin. Her face was framed in a hole cut in the top bag, and the corners of it were fastened back so it made a bullet shape around her head and shoulders. She'd done a similar thing at the bottom – her feet, in grubby old trainers, sticking out from two holes. And there were two holes at the side for her arms.

'Er . . . what are you, Kit?' William asked at last.

'Can't you guess?' They shook their heads.

'I'm a slug!'

'A *slug*?' Rosie repeated.

'Yes, look – here's my trail of slime,' she said brightly, turning to show a long length of clingfilm fastened to the back behind her feet, trailing along the floor.

'Slime, eh?' said Tim, slowly.

'*Mmm . . . oh-kay*,' said Rosie dubiously.

They stood back to let Kitty shuffle into the living-room, and exchanged glances. What on earth did she think she was playing at? There's nothing magical about slugs!

William's mum and sister looked equally surprised, but William jabbed Sally in the ribs when she started to speak. He didn't want Kitty's feelings hurt.

'Let's play Pass the Parcel,' he called out cheerfully, and soon the children were sitting in a circle playing the old game they all loved. Tim won that, and Rosie won Musical Statues, which followed. Kitty made them all laugh, the way she had to hop and shuffle about, trailing her 'slime'. In fact, even when she did something simple like grabbing a sandwich they all fell about in great gales of laughter. The wizard, the vampire, the fairy and the witches all agreed that the slug was the funniest thing ever.

'Mum usually hates slugs in the garden,' William said, 'but not now!' Kitty beamed.

'And you haven't seen my magic trick yet,' she said mysteriously.

Next they played the memory game,

where you have to memorise things laid out on a tray. Anita was the best. They played 'I packed my bag and in it I put . . .' where each of them added something to the contents of the bag, so the list got harder to remember as it got longer.

'I packed my bag and in it I put – a spell book, a spider, a toad, a wand, a cauldron, an imp, a bag of magic stones, a mouse, a fortune-teller's ball, a magic mirror, a star, a . . . oh, what's next?' cried Rosie.

'A toadstool! You're out, Rosie,' said Melissa, gleefully, 'I win this time!'

'It's not fair!' muttered the slug – but not seriously. Just then the doorbell rang. 'That'll be Dan,' Kitty said with a grin.

When her brother came into the room they saw he was carrying Kitty's embroidered bedspread. It had been a birthday present from Anita and her family, and twinkled with mirrors.

'Now it's time for my magic!' Kitty announced.

Dan asked Sally to hold one end of the bedspread and William to hold the other, so that it made a kind of screen across one end of the room. He told them to look straight ahead and not peep, as he and Kitty disappeared behind it. Then William's mother played the CD he'd brought – and the room was filled with tinkling, whooshing music that sounded like the sea, the wind and the sky, all at once. There was a rustling and some whispering from behind the bedspread.

'What's going on?' whispered Rosie to Tim. All the children felt strangely excited.

At last Daniel came out. Standing to one side he said in a loud voice, 'Ladies and gentlemen, what you didn't know was – that slug was a magic slug. Once upon a time a wicked monster put a spell on

Kitty's Friends

her, and said it would only be taken off if people learned to like her, despite her sliminess. Well, that has happened tonight, and so I present to you . . . the slug's true self! Drop the bedspread, please!'

And there stood the most bewitching
angelic creature they had ever seen. Kitty
had brushed her hair for once, sprinkled it
with glitter, and topped it with an Alice
band on which she had stuck a halo, made
from cardboard covered in silver foil. She
wore a long white nightdress (one of her
mum's) with a silver tinsel belt, which
matched the tinsel bracelets which caught

the bottom of her sleeves. Best of all were the wings. With the help of her dad she'd made a harness from wire coat-hangers, which fitted around her shoulders and supported a pair of wonderful long cardboard wings, painted light grey with a mass of individual feathers beautifully drawn with a broad silver marker pen. Kitty's feet were bare and she held her hands out, palms up.

'Ohhh!' said Rosie, Anita and Mel in chorus.

'Kitty's a little angel,' said William.

When they'd finished clapping, Tim asked, 'How did you do that?'

'It was all under her slug costume,' said Dan. 'All I had to do was help her fold out the wings and make the halo stand up.'

'Brilliant idea,' said Sally, 'but why an angel?'

'Angels are magic creatures, of course,' said Kitty. 'I read in a book that all sorts

of people believe in them. So I thought I'd
be one!'

By the time they'd finished admiring
her, and eating and drinking, and
laughing amongst themselves, the doorbell
started to ring again. One by one, William
led in Tim's mum, Kitty's parents (carrying
Baby Tom), Anita's whole family, Melissa's
mum and dad, and finally, Rosie's mum
and sister Sara. They were all nicely
dressed, as if for a special event.

'I thought we'd extend this party!' said
William's mum. 'Cheer us *all* up!'

They opened a couple of bottles of fizzy
wine, and Sally fetched more cola and
apple juice from the fridge. Kitty's dad put
some cans of beer on the table. There were
plenty of snacks for everybody, and they
talked and laughed as they ate. Sally put
on a CD of chart hits and after a while,
Sara and Sally began to dance, and Rosie
and her mum joined in, then Kitty's

Kitty's Friends

parents too. Auntie Susan held Baby Tom, who made happy gurgling noises and waved William's wand around, like a baby wizard.

Kitty and friends

Tim kept pretending to be a vampire, making Anita's little brothers run away and squeal, whilst the two witches joined in the dancing with the fairy. The whole atmosphere was . . . magical.

But every time William looked at Kitty he started to laugh – even more than when she'd been a slug.

'Why do you keep getting the giggles, William?' she asked.

'It's just the thought of you being a little angel . . . *you* of all people!' he spluttered. 'It's such a . . . such a . . . oh, what's the word?'

'*Transformation!*' said Kitty, triumphantly. 'And Will, the whole point is, you've always got to believe it's possible. That's the real magic – don't you see?'